Make friends with

Sheltie

The little pony with the big heart

Sheltie is the lovable little Shetland pony with a big personality. His best friend and owner is Emma, and together they have lots of exciting adventures.

Share Sheltie and Emma's adventures in

SHELTIE THE SHETLAND PONY
SHELTIE SAVES THE DAY
SHELTIE AND THE RUNAWAY
SHELTIE FINDS A FRIEND
SHELTIE TO THE RESCUE
SHELTIE IN DANGER
SHELTIE RIDES TO WIN
SHELTIE AND THE SADDLE MYSTERY
SHELTIE LEADS THE WAY
SHELTIE THE HERO
SHELTIE IN TROUBLE
SHELTIE AND THE STRAY
SHELTIE AND THE SNOW PONY

Peter Clover was born and went to school in London. He was a storyboard artist and illustrator before he began to put words to his pictures. He enjoys painting, travelling, cooking and keeping fit, and lives on the coast in Somerset.

Also by Peter Clover in Puffin

The Sheltie series

Sheltie on Parade

Peter Clover

PUFFIN BOOKS

For Sandra and David

PUFFIN BOOKS

Published by the Penguin Group
Penguin Books Ltd, 27 Wrights Lane, London W8 5TZ, England
Penguin Putnam Inc., 375 Hudson Street, New York, New York 10014, USA
Penguin Books Australia Ltd, Ringwood, Victoria, Australia
Penguin Books Canada Ltd, 10 Alcorn Avenue, Toronto, Ontario, Canada M4V 3B2
Penguin Books (NZ) Ltd, Private Bag 102902, NSMC, Auckland, New Zealand

Penguin Books Ltd, Registered Offices: Harmondsworth, Middlesex, England

First published 1999
1 3 5 7 9 10 8 6 4 2

Created by Working Partners Ltd, London, W12 7QY

The moral right of the author has been asserted

Set in 14/22 Palatino

Made and printed in England by Clays Ltd, St Ives plc

British Library Cataloguing in Publication Data
A CIP catalogue record for this book is available from the British Library

ISBN 0–141–30449–9

Chapter One

It was the first day of the half-term holidays. Emma was looking forward to a week of riding Sheltie, her little Shetland pony, all over Little Applewood.

'One whole week of riding all day and every day,' Emma whispered softly in Sheltie's ear. Then she scooped his breakfast of pony mix into the feed manger.

'One scoop for a hungry pony and a tiny extra handful for half-term,' she laughed. 'You're going to need lots of energy for what I've got planned!'

Sheltie tossed his head and whinnied his approval. Sheltie always had heaps of energy. But he never refused any extra treats or titbits.

The little pony pushed past Emma and aimed his nose into the feed manger. Then he gobbled down every last bit of pony mix. When he had finished, he looked up, licked his lips and nodded his head as if to say, 'Right, then. I'm ready for anything.'

Emma tacked up Sheltie in record time and was soon riding him at a steady walk up the lane. They were off to meet Sally and her pony, Minnow, from Fox Hall Manor. Then they were going to have a mounted meeting and plan seven days of fun.

Emma had already thought of lots of things to do. A picnic, a day patrolling the downs, and a visit to Mrs Warner, an old lady who lived alone on the moor. Then she thought of a group ride with all her friends who had ponies of their own, and maybe practising jumping in Sally's back meadow. Sally had a small course of jumps set up, and the two girls liked to pretend they were champion showjumpers competing at a big event.

'I wonder what Sally has thought

of,' said Emma. But Sheltie wasn't listening. He was more interested in what was going on outside Mr Crock's cottage, further up the lane.

Mr Crock and his old friend Fred Berry were standing out in the lane. And they seemed to be fighting. Emma couldn't believe her eyes. Both Mr Crock and Fred Berry were waving wooden swords and jabbing at each other with them.

'Take that, you scoundrel!' yelled Mr Crock.

'Missed, you old fool!' laughed Fred Berry. 'It will take at least three of you to win the Prince's Crown.'

'Quick, Sheltie!' urged Emma. She hurried the little pony into a fast trot and dashed up the lane to stop the

two men before they hurt each
other.

She raced right up to them and
jumped from the saddle. Sheltie blew a
loud raspberry as Emma forced her
way between the two men and pushed
them apart.

'It's the Black Knight come to save

you,' laughed Fred, and Mr Crock's face broke into a broad grin.

'Fear not, Black Knight,' smiled Mr Crock. 'I'll make mincemeat of him on my own if he will only stand still.'

Emma suddenly realized that Mr Crock and Fred were only play-acting. At first she felt really silly for trying to break up their game. But then she saw how funny it must have seemed and burst out laughing.

'Aren't you two a bit old to be playing with toy swords?' she smiled.

'We're not playing,' said Mr Crock. 'We're practising.'

'Practising?' said Emma. 'What for?'

'So we'll be the champions of the tournament,' grinned Fred.

'Tournament?' said Emma. 'What tournament?'

'Haven't you heard, Emma? The Bicklington Battlers are touring the countryside. They haven't been in these parts for years and years. And now they're coming to put on a tournament in Little Applewood!'

'The Bicklington Battlers?' repeated Emma. 'Who are *they*?'

Sheltie cocked his head to one side as if wondering what they were all saying.

'They're Knights of the Round Table,' said Mr Crock.

'Subjects of the legendary Prince John,' added Fred Berry. 'Well, actors really,' he said. 'People who roam the countryside putting wrongs to right.'

7

'Wrongs to right?' puzzled Emma. She was a little confused.

'The actors dress up as medieval knights, and re-enact historic scenes and battles that took place across the country,' explained Mr Crock.

'And a famous battle took place right here in Little Applewood, hundreds of years ago,' added Fred.

Emma could hardly believe what she was hearing. It sounded too fantastic.

'And the best part,' said Mr Crock, 'is that they will be looking for "extras" to make the performance seem more realistic.'

'There might even be television cameras and everything,' said Fred. Then he raised his wooden sword

above his head and aimed a sneaky
blow at his old friend.

'The Prince's Champion,' he cried,
before Mr Crock stepped aside and
knocked the sword out of Fred's hand.

Sheltie lunged forward and lifted up
the wooden sword in his mouth. He

held it firmly in his teeth and blew through his nostrils.

'Sheltie wants to play too,' laughed Mr Crock.

Sheltie held the sword high and shook his mane.

'I bet he'd easily get a part in the parade,' said Fred.

'Parade!' echoed Emma. She was very interested in parades.

'Oh yes,' said Mr Crock. 'There's always a grand parade after the battle.' He told Emma that there was a poster pinned to the village green notice-board, advertising for mounted soldiers, footmen, handmaidens and followers.

'Haven't you seen it?' asked Fred Berry.

Emma shook her head. Sheltie copied Emma and shook his head too.

'No, we haven't seen anything,' answered Emma. But she couldn't wait to get to the village green to have a look!

Chapter Two

Emma and Sheltie stood in front of the noticeboard.

'Coming soon,' read Emma. Sheltie cocked his head to one side, listening.

'The Bicklington Battlers,' she continued, 'will perform a spectacular jousting tournament in Little Applewood, re-enacting a historical battle which took place here in medieval times. Anyone wishing to take part in the grand parade after the battle should attend the auditions on the village green at three o'clock on Tuesday. All ponies especially welcome.'

Sheltie blew a loud snort and flicked his ears.

'*All ponies especially welcome.* That means us!' said Emma. 'We're going to

be in the grand parade, Sheltie! A mounted knight on a trusty steed. I can't wait!'

Emma rode on to Sally's as quickly as she could. She wanted to tell her best friend all about the grand parade. But Emma was surprised to discover that Sally already knew all about it.

'I only found out at breakfast,' said Sally. 'Daddy showed me the notice in his newspaper. There was a big advertisement about the Bicklington Battlers and a piece announcing the auditions for the grand parade. Isn't it fantastic?'

Sally sat upright in Minnow's saddle and tried to make herself as tall as possible. 'Do you think I'll make a good mounted soldier?' she asked.

14

'We'll both make *great* soldiers,' laughed Emma. Sheltie nuzzled into Minnow and nibbled at his mane.

'If we're not chosen for mounted soldiers, perhaps we could be footmen or something,' said Sally.

'We'll be mounted soldiers or nothing,' said Emma. '*And* we'll be at the head of the parade. You'll see!'

Sally grinned. When Emma was this determined, almost nothing could stop her.

Suddenly, all they could think about was the Bicklington Battlers and the grand parade. All their other plans about picnics and patrolling the downs were forgotten.

'We've only got tomorrow to get ready,' said Emma.

'That's plenty of time,' said Sally.

'It's *not*,' scowled Emma. 'It's enough time for you and Minnow. But look at Sheltie. We're going to need at least a week to get him ready.'

Sheltie looked up and belched. His long, hairy mane was untidy and straggly. His forelock hung over his eyes and his thick coat needed a good brush. Emma had groomed him thoroughly only three days earlier, but Sheltie had been rolling in the brambles and was looking a little scruffy.

He pushed his soft velvet muzzle into Emma's hand and blew a soft whicker. Sheltie couldn't help looking the way he did. He always looked like that. Emma tried as best she could to

keep Sheltie neat and tidy, but
somehow he always managed to undo
all her efforts.

Emma didn't care though. She loved
Sheltie just the way he was.

'I'll give you a hand if you like,' said Sally.

Emma smiled. 'That's very nice, but I think Sheltie is my job. You tend to Minnow and I'll get Sheltie shipshape for the audition.'

They spent the rest of the day riding through the countryside above Little Applewood. All they could talk about was winning two places in the grand parade.

'I might even plait a ribbon into Minnow's tail,' said Sally.

Emma smiled. The thought of plaiting a ribbon into Sheltie's tail made her laugh.

'If I did that to Sheltie, you would never see the ribbon,' she said. 'His tail is so bushy.'

Sally agreed. 'Sheltie looks best with just a good brush. I love the way his mane and forelock go all floppy just after you've groomed him. And how his long tail becomes silky and falls almost to the ground. I've never seen another pony's tail do that!'

It was true. After a good grooming session, Sheltie could look spectacular.

Emma made up her mind to start Sheltie's grooming programme bright and early the following morning. Sheltie was going to be the best turned out pony at the audition. And the most handsome pony in the whole parade.

Chapter Three

The next day, Emma was crossing the paddock by eight o'clock. Sheltie had already been watered and fed and was now standing to attention as Emma approached with brushes and combs.

After an hour, Emma said, 'There, Sheltie! Now you look at least half tidy.'

Emma brushed out the last strands of Sheltie's tail and stood back to admire her handiwork. Sheltie's mane lay neatly across his neck and his light chestnut coat shone like silk in the morning sunlight.

'Just wait till they see *you*,' said Emma. 'The Bicklington Battlers won't be able to place you anywhere except right at the front of the parade!'

Sheltie flicked his freshly combed tail and blew a cheeky snort. He seemed to know that he looked very fine indeed.

Emma continued with Sheltie's grooming. She cleaned and picked out his hoofs then applied hoof oil until they gleamed as though they had been freshly varnished. She polished his tack and gave him one final rub down with a dry sponge.

21

When Emma had finished, Sheltie looked terrific . . . In fact, he looked spectacular. A little Shetland pony star. It had taken Emma all morning, but it was worth it.

'You've done a fantastic job,' said Mum. 'I've never seen Sheltie look so neat and tidy.'

Emma thought Sheltie looked

brilliant. But this wasn't the Sheltie she was used to. Secretly, she preferred him when he was scruffy, with his unruly mane sticking up all over the place.

Sheltie didn't care though. He didn't seem to mind *what* he looked like. Having fun was all Sheltie thought about.

Emma checked her watch. It was nearly lunchtime. Her main worry was keeping Sheltie neat and tidy until three o'clock when the auditions were being held on the village green.

She left Sheltie in the paddock with a stern warning before she went in for a drink and a sandwich.

'Now, be very, very good,' said Emma. 'And no rolling!'

Sheltie peered at Emma through his freshly brushed forelock. He looked so innocent with his big brown eyes. But Emma didn't trust him one bit. She knew that she only had to turn her back for two minutes and Sheltie could be up to all kinds of mischief.

Emma hurried her lunch then went back out to the paddock, where a big surprise was waiting for her. Sheltie was standing in exactly the same spot where Emma had left him. And the little pony didn't have one hair out of place.

Emma was so pleased that she palmed Sheltie a peppermint treat. Then she sat on the paddock rail and gave his special Sunday saddle one last polish with a clean duster.

Sheltie stood with his fuzzy chin resting on Emma's knee. He knew that the saddle meant they were going somewhere. Sheltie flicked his tail excitedly and waited.

Ten minutes later, Emma was riding

him down the lane to meet up with Sally and Minnow.

Emma and Sally were going for a little ride before the auditions.

Both girls had set their sights on being mounted soldiers and Emma shivered with excitement at the thought.

The afternoon was bright and sunny with big, white, cotton-wool clouds rolling in from the downs. Emma checked her wristwatch. She would be meeting Sally in fifteen minutes.

'I wonder who else will be there!' said Emma.

Sheltie pricked up his ears. But he wasn't listening to Emma. Sheltie had heard something else – the patter of

delicate hoofs dancing down the lane
behind him.

Sheltie turned his head to look and
Emma twisted round in the saddle.
She had heard something too!

Chapter Four

The dancing hoofs belonged to
Clementine, Marjorie Wallace's pet
goat. Marjorie Wallace was a friendly
old lady who lived in a cottage at the
foot of Beacon Hill. She had nine cats
and found homes for all kinds of
unwanted animals. Clementine the
goat lived in a field at the back of
Marjorie's cottage. She had obviously
escaped.

Clementine's hoofs clattered on the loose stones as she jigged and pranced, only metres away. In her mouth she held the remains of a freshly plucked flower. *Gulp!* Emma watched the flower disappear.

'Clementine!' exclaimed Emma. 'What on earth are you doing out all on your own?'

Sheltie blew a friendly raspberry and Clementine answered with a bleat.

Emma noticed the chewed rope hanging from Clementine's collar. Marjorie's goat had obviously bitten through her tether and decided to go walkabout-eatabout.

'Come on,' said Emma. 'I'd better take you home.'

Clementine cocked her head to one side and stared at Sheltie. She remembered the little pony from his visits to the cottage. Clementine jigged up to Sheltie and gave his rump a friendly butt with her short horns.

Emma took the opportunity to grab Clementine's rope. Soon she was leading the funny goat along the lane to Beacon Hill. She glanced at her watch again and hoped that Sally would wait for her.

It didn't take long to deliver Clementine to Marjorie's cottage. The old lady was very grateful to Emma. It turned out that Clementine had been escaping quite a lot recently.

While Emma watched Marjorie attach Clementine to her running line, Sheltie trotted across to the back paddock to say hello to Mudlark and Sophie, Marjorie's two donkeys.

Mudlark threw his head back with a loud hee-haw when he saw Sheltie, and the little pony joined in with a shrill whinny.

'Listen to those two,' laughed Marjorie. 'You'd think they hadn't seen each other for years!'

Emma laughed too. But not for long.

The next thing Sheltie did was something he always did when he was happy. Sheltie started to roll on the ground.

'Oh no!' shrieked Emma. But it was too late to stop him. Sheltie was already on his back with his legs

kicking the air, wallowing in the mud and dirt.

Emma rushed across and grabbed at Sheltie's reins. The little Shetland pony jiggled to his feet and looked at Emma as if to say, 'That was fun, wasn't it?'

Emma was really upset. She huffed a big sigh and said, 'Oh, just look at you now, Sheltie. You're all messy! And we've got the auditions in an hour.'

'He doesn't look too bad,' said Marjorie.

'Yes, he does,' argued Emma. 'He looks terrible!'

Sheltie shook out the dust from his mane then tried to nibble the flowers on Marjorie's dress.

'Stop it, Sheltie. You've been so good all morning up until now!'

Sheltie stopped immediately and looked up at Emma with an innocent expression on his face.

Emma could never stay cross with Sheltie for long. When he looked at her with those big brown eyes, her heart always melted and she forgave him instantly.

'Come on. Let's just hope Sally is still waiting,' said Emma. 'You'll have to do, just as you are.' She leaped into Sheltie's saddle and urged him into a trot. 'Bye, Marjorie,' she called over her shoulder. 'We've got to dash.'

They cantered back down the lane on drumming hoofs and met up with

34

Sally and Minnow at the little stone
bridge crossing the stream.

Sally was dressed in her best riding
clothes and Minnow looked
magnificent. His piebald coat gleamed
in the sunshine and his fine silky mane
fell neatly to the side of his neck.

When Sally saw the state of Sheltie
she pulled a face.

'Sorry we're late,' said Emma. 'We
had to return a runaway goat. And
Sheltie's been up to his favourite trick
– rolling!'

Sally could see that Emma was
flustered and upset.

'It doesn't matter,' said Sally. 'Even
if Sheltie is a little muddy.'

'A *little* muddy!' exclaimed Emma.
'He's really messy. And he looked so

smart and tidy ten minutes ago.'

Sheltie blew a loud raspberry. He didn't care about the mud. And neither did Emma really. But she wanted him to look extra special for the audition, and there was no hope of that now. There was no time for a ride either, so they hurried on to the village.

Chapter Five

The audition on the village green was being organized by a large, busy lady in a pink hat. Most of the village had turned out and was ready to parade past the audition station set up in the middle of the green.

Everyone who had a pony was there, well groomed and excited about winning a place in the parade.

Those people without ponies had

been organized into small groups and were waiting patiently. Mr Crock and Fred Berry stood to attention, side by side, still clutching their wooden swords. Both wore huge grins.

'We've already been chosen to be marching foot soldiers,' said Mr Crock proudly.

Emma smiled. She saw her friend Tracy Diamond with her pony, Blaze, and gave a little wave. Then she saw Alice Parker on Blue and gave her the thumbs up. But when Emma caught sight of snooty Melody Parker on Sapphire, her face fell.

Melody was Alice Parker's cousin and a real troublemaker. Emma didn't like her at all. She was a selfish spoilsport.

Melody Parker had seen Emma and Sheltie too, and was already laughing. Emma saw her whisper something to her equally snooty brother, Simon, and felt her face flush hot and red.

The large lady in the pink hat was called Mrs Brandon. She shouted to Emma and Sally and motioned for

them to come over and walk Sheltie and Minnow past the table at which she was sitting.

Minnow was very well behaved and walked past perfectly with his head high. Mrs Brandon smiled and made a note on her clipboard.

'Just what we're looking for,' she announced. 'A second escort to walk alongside Prince John at the head of the parade. The pony's colouring is perfect.'

Sally gasped with pride – 'A second escort!'

Then she heard Mrs Brandon telling someone who the other escort was going to be. It was Melody Parker on Sapphire. Sally didn't like Melody either. Nobody did.

Sally pulled a face at Emma. But at least she was going to have a leading part in the grand parade.

Sally crossed her fingers for Emma and held them up for her friend to see.

Next, Mrs Brandon addressed Emma and Sheltie. Their ride past was not as controlled as Sally and Minnow's.

It started out well, but Sheltie suddenly became more interested in a squirrel clinging to the trunk of a large oak tree. He kept trying to lunge over towards it to make friends.

Emma did the best she could but Sheltie kept fidgeting and jangling his bit. He tossed his head constantly, and his walk past was more of a zigzag than a straight line.

'Oh dear,' said Mrs Brandon. 'I can see the little fellow is quite a character, but you seem to be having trouble controlling him!'

'He's not normally like this,' pleaded Emma. 'Usually, he's very well behaved!'

'That may be true,' said Mrs Brandon, 'but he might let us all down on the day. We can't risk spoiling the grand parade. I'll put you down as a handmaiden and you can leave your pony at home.'

'A handmaiden!' cried Emma. 'I don't want to be a handmaiden. I want to be a mounted soldier on Sheltie.'

'Can't they be jesters or clowns?' yelled Melody Parker. 'That's all they're fit for. They look so funny.' She roared with laughter and Emma felt really annoyed.

Sheltie blew a loud snort and Emma set her mouth in a firm line. Then Mrs Brandon said, 'That's not such a bad idea! After all, a mounted court jester entertaining the crowds from the rear of the parade would make a perfect finish. And we've never done that before. It will be a first!' She seemed very pleased with the idea.

Emma wasn't so sure. She didn't like the thought of everyone laughing at her and Sheltie. Especially horrible Melody Parker.

Back at the cottage, Mum had a talk with Emma while Sally played with Joshua, Emma's little brother.

'Try to think of it as a starring role,' smiled Mum. 'After all, there will only be *one* court jester. And after the parade has passed you'll be the last one everybody sees. You can entertain the crowds.'

'But everyone will be laughing at me. What can I do to be entertaining?' asked Emma.

'I'm sure you'll think of something,' said Mum kindly. 'I'm sure the crowds won't be laughing *at* you. I'll make you and Sheltie both grand costumes. After all it's a big event for Little Applewood. And you do want to be in it. Don't you?'

Emma nodded feebly.

'But I wanted to be at the front with Prince John and Sally,' she said.

'I'd rather be at the back with you and Sheltie, Emma,' said Sally, 'than up at the front next to Melody Parker.'

Suddenly it didn't seem such a bad idea after all.

'You can do it,' Sally added. 'You and Sheltie always make me laugh and I bet everyone will join in. Sheltie's so funny.'

Emma brightened a little. 'Yes, I suppose he is,' she smiled.

Emma and Sally suddenly burst out laughing at the idea of Sheltie being a clown.

'There,' said Mum. 'That sounds a lot better, doesn't it?'

It was true, thought Emma. Perhaps it wouldn't be so bad after all.

Chapter Six

There were only three days left to the big day. Prince John's Tournament was going to take place at three o'clock on Saturday afternoon in Mr Brown's top meadow. And afterwards, the grand parade would march through Little Applewood.

Mum started work on Emma's and Sheltie's costumes right away. Everyone else would be borrowing outfits from the theatre company, but Mum was making Emma's and Sheltie's especially for them. There was to be a dress rehearsal for the parade on Thursday evening. Emma hoped that the costumes would be finished in time!

The more she thought about it, the more Emma became excited about riding Sheltie in the grand parade. She forgot all about Melody Parker. Anyway, as Mum kept reminding her, Melody would be at the front and Emma wouldn't even see her.

Wednesday passed quickly, and on Thursday, Mum worked all day to finish Emma's and Sheltie's costumes.

Emma couldn't wait to try hers on. Mum had made Emma a bright tunic in shiny red and yellow material. She had some dazzling green and gold leggings and a black and red striped waistcoat with lots of little bells sewn on to it.

Mum had even made a three-pointed jester's cap to fit over Emma's riding hat. Each point of the cap had its own little bell sewn on to the tip. When Emma nodded her head, or moved it from side to side, all the bells tinkled at once.

Sheltie's costume was made like a pony rug, in the same red and yellow material. It covered his whole body completely and almost hung down to the ground.

Mum had made him a headdress too: a big fluffy feather sewn on to a

headband, which danced between his
ears and bobbed up and down when
he trotted round the paddock.

Mum had copied Sheltie's costume
from another poster she had seen,
showing Prince John on his charger,
Casper.

Emma was thrilled to bits. Sheltie
seemed to like the costumes too and
snorted his approval.

'They're fantastic, Mum,' said Emma.

Joshua stood on the bottom rail of the wooden fence and watched wide-eyed as Emma rode Sheltie round and round the paddock. He held his arm up in the air and yelled 'Charge!' Sheltie looked just like one of his toys.

Emma galloped on Sheltie from one end of the paddock to the other. And Mum held Joshua up high as they cheered and cheered.

'Just wait until Sally sees us,' laughed Emma.

'You'll be the best-dressed pair in the parade,' smiled Mum.

Emma wanted to ride to the top meadow, where the parade started, with Sheltie in his full costume, but

Mum thought it might be best if he
only wore the feather headdress for
the rehearsal.

'You never know,' said Mum.
'Something might happen, and we
don't want to spoil it for Saturday.'

Emma knew exactly what Mum
meant. Sheltie might get his costume
muddy or, worse still, decide to roll

while he was wearing it and ruin everything.

'Let's save it for the day,' added Mum, 'and get Sheltie used to wearing it here in the paddock first.'

Emma thought that was a good idea. Sheltie didn't seem to mind wearing his costume. But he did keep stopping to look back at all the material flapping in the wind behind him.

Mum helped Emma to take Sheltie's costume off and folded it neatly over her arm.

'I'll bring Joshua to watch the rehearsal,' she said, 'and I'll take Sheltie's costume to show Mrs Brandon what he'll really look like on Saturday.'

They set off almost immediately, Mum and Joshua on foot, and met several people on their way to the top meadow.

Mr Crock and Fred Berry were walking along wearing cloaks and battle helmets. They had realistic plastic swords now and still kept jabbing at each other playfully as they sauntered along.

'They're worse than a couple of kids,' laughed Mum. Mr Crock and Fred Berry were really enjoying themselves.

They met Alice Parker and her pony, Blue, as they crossed the meadow. Then they saw Sally leading Minnow down from the top field. She was dressed as a page in a smart black and

white costume and waving a long
banner.

'You look great,' said Sally when
they finally met.

'And so do you,' smiled Emma. 'I
like the banner!'

'Mum made it for Prince John,' Sally
explained.

Sheltie lunged forward and tried to catch the end of the flowing material in his teeth.

'Stop that, Sheltie,' giggled Emma. 'Behave!'

Sheltie turned his head quickly and sent his headdress wonky. It slipped down and tickled his nose. He gave an enormous snort and Mum laughed.

As Mum straightened the headdress, Mrs Brandon came over. Mum was showing off Sheltie's costume to her as more members of the parade began to arrive. Quite a crowd had gathered now.

Emma didn't notice Melody Parker suddenly ride up on Sapphire. Emma didn't realize it was her straight away because she was dressed in her page's costume. It was the same black and white costume as Sally's.

Then Melody spoke in her snooty way. 'Doesn't Shorty look funny with a feather sticking out of his head?' and Emma recognized her voice immediately.

'Mind you,' added Melody, 'he'd look much better if you put a bag over his head!'

Then she took a swipe with her hand and tried to grab the feather from Sheltie's headdress.

Fortunately, Sheltie saw it coming and skipped sideways as Melody reached across. This made Melody lean further than she intended and she slid clumsily from Sapphire's saddle.

She landed on the grass with a

bump and Emma giggled. Serves you right, Melody! thought Emma.

Mum and Mrs Brandon spun round to see what was happening. Joshua was giggling too.

'What's going on here?' asked Mrs Brandon.

'It was Shorty, not me,' grumbled

Melody. 'He took a nip at Sapphire and upset my balance.'

'That's rubbish,' said Sally, coming to Sheltie's defence. 'You were just causing trouble as usual, Melody Parker. And it's your own fault.'

Melody gathered Sapphire's reins and glared at Sally.

'I'll get you for that, Sally Jones!' she muttered under her breath so none of the grown-ups could hear.

Sally looked uncomfortable, but didn't say anything. It was Mrs Brandon who spoke up. 'I don't want any more fooling around from any of you,' she said sternly. 'There are plenty of others who would love the opportunity of riding in the parade. So no more nonsense!'

Emma opened her mouth to say something but decided not to. Sheltie said it for her and blew a loud raspberry at Melody's back.

'Does he always do that?' asked Mrs Brandon.

'Only when he's enjoying himself,' said Mum. She gave Emma a wink, and Joshua giggled even more.

'Well, Sheltie certainly seems to amuse the little ones,' Mrs Brandon added. 'I think he's going to be a very popular addition to the parade.'

Melody remounted quickly and trotted away without as much as a backward glance.

Chapter Seven

It took half an hour to organize everyone into their positions for the procession. Prince John, in his suit of armour at the head of the parade, looked magnificent on Casper.

His two escorts were on either side of him: Sally on Minnow and Melody on Sapphire. Prince John carried a long flowing banner with the words 'Bicklington Battlers' embroidered in gold on the deep-green material.

Then came the band, and behind them trotted two rows of mounted knights, four ponies deep, followed by Prince John's army of foot soldiers.

Mr Crock and Fred Berry marched

tall and proud in their uniforms. Behind the soldiers came the handmaidens and grooms, followed by a few mounted villagers in period costume. Then, last of all, came the court jester, Emma on Sheltie.

Sheltie was enjoying every minute of the rehearsal and he lifted his little hoofs high with each step he took. Mrs Brandon had given Emma a red balloon on a small stick to wave.

The procession marched right round the top meadow in perfect formation. Emma glowed with excitement thinking about Saturday.

When Mrs Brandon was satisfied with everything, the parade broke up and everyone went home.

'Remember your positions,' Mrs

Brandon called to the departing groups. 'And be here in good time for three o'clock Saturday to watch the big battle. Thank you, everyone, and goodbye until then.' Her voice trailed off into the light summer breeze.

At teatime, Emma told Dad all about the rehearsal in the top meadow.

'And everyone marched round and round and I waved my balloon and Sheltie was brilliant,' said Emma, all in one breath.

'I don't think you're going to sleep a wink for the next two nights!' laughed Dad.

Emma was already breathless with excitement just retelling the afternoon's events.

'I think I'll video the whole extravaganza,' said Dad brightly.

'Oh, that would be great,' said Emma. 'And make sure you take lots of film of me and Sheltie.'

'I'll try and save a tiny bit of film and record you and Sheltie at the end,' said Dad seriously.

Emma's face fell.

Dad burst out laughing. 'Only joking. I'll film lots and lots of you and Sheltie.'

That night, what Dad had said was true. Emma could hardly sleep a wink. All she could think about was Saturday and the grand parade. But finally she closed her eyes and dreamed of riding Sheltie in the procession with the crowds whistling and cheering for her as they rode through Little Applewood.

Saturday couldn't come round quickly enough. And when it did, Emma and Sheltie spent the morning out riding with Sally and Minnow. Sally said she was looking forward to the parade in the afternoon but she was a bit worried about Melody.

'What if she starts making trouble,' complained Sally.

'Don't you worry about *her*,' said Emma defiantly. 'Don't let Melody Parker spoil your fun. She's always making trouble. But don't forget, you'll have Prince John and his giant horse in between you. So she can't *do* anything, can she?'

'I know,' answered Sally. 'But she's so horrible. I wish it was you and Sheltie up at the front, instead of Melody.'

Emma would have liked that too. But nevertheless, she was looking forward to being in the parade and entertaining the crowds from the back.

After lunch, Emma spent an hour grooming Sheltie. Even though most of the little pony would be hidden under his costume, she wanted him to look his best. Emma paid extra attention to the bits of Sheltie that *would* be showing – his mane, hoofs and tail. By the time Emma had finished brushing and combing, both Sheltie's mane and tail were bigger and bushier than ever. Then she oiled

his hoofs until they shone like satin.

'Right,' said Emma. 'You're ready.'

Sheltie shook the silky fringe out of his eyes. Suddenly it seemed twice as long as before. Then he looked back at the huge cloud of tail that billowed behind him in the breeze as if to say, 'Where did that come from?'

Emma was really pleased with her

efforts and ran to fetch Mum and Dad. They were going to fix Sheltie's costume for her while she went upstairs to change.

When Emma came back out to the paddock, dressed in her jester's outfit, Sheltie was ready and waiting.

Mum was holding Joshua in Sheltie's saddle. And Joshua was staring at the big red feather stuck on top of Sheltie's head. Each time Sheltie moved, the feather swayed from side to side.

'Come on, Joshua, off you get,' said Mum. 'Emma and Sheltie have got to go now.'

Joshua clapped his hands and waved as Emma rode Sheltie away up the lane.

'See you at the tournament,' Emma called over her shoulder. She waved her balloon on a stick, which she had tied to her wrist with a loop of string, and all the bells on her hat tinkled as she turned her head. 'Don't forget to video us in the parade, Dad.'

'I won't,' he promised.

Sheltie broke into a trot and his brightly coloured costume swished and flowed with every step.

Chapter Eight

When Emma and Sheltie arrived at the top meadow, they were surprised at the number of people already there. A huge crowd had turned up for the event.

A large arena in the middle of the meadow had been roped off for the tournament.

Coloured flags and bunting decorated the area. And people sat all around it on blankets and rugs, eagerly awaiting the show.

There were plenty of people in costume too, ready for the parade. And lots and lots of riders on ponies. But none looked quite as special as Emma and Sheltie.

Sally and Minnow were already there. 'I didn't spot you and Sheltie straight away,' said Sally. 'There are so many colourful costumes. But I recognized Sheltie by his size and then saw his feather waving. You two look great.'

'So do you,' said Emma. 'Have you seen what's-her-face yet?' she asked. She was determined not to mention Melody Parker's name.

'No,' answered Sally, 'but I expect

73

she'll be here any minute.' And suddenly, there she was, riding Sapphire round and round inside the roped off arena.

'Look at her, showing off,' said Emma.

'Yes, but at least it's keeping her out of trouble,' said Sally. 'And you must admit, she *is* a good rider.'

While they were waiting for the Bicklington Battlers, several others joined Melody in the ring. At least ten riders in costume were putting their ponies through their paces – walking, trotting, cantering and generally performing a little show of their own for the admiring crowd.

The audience grew larger as more

people arrived and settled themselves down.

'Shall we go and join in?' suggested Emma. 'It looks like fun.'

'But Melody's there,' worried Sally. 'Do you think it's a good idea?'

'Why not?' said Emma. '*She* doesn't own the ring, does she? We can't keep away from her for ever.'

'Come on then,' said Sally.

When Emma and Sheltie trotted into the ring, the whole crowd clapped and cheered. Melody Parker spun round in the saddle to see what the applause was about. Sally was pleased that no one had seemed to notice *her* on Minnow.

Melody quickly trotted over.

'Hello, Emma. Is that Shorty under that lot or is it a sheep?' she said sarcastically.

Emma was furious. 'You'll never change, will you, Melody?'

Melody looked taken aback. 'I have tried to be nice to you and Sally.'

'Oh no you haven't!' said Emma.

'Is it too late to start now then?' smiled Melody mischievously. She held out her hand for Emma to shake in a bid of friendship. But instead Melody suddenly grabbed Emma's balloon and deliberately burst it.

The balloon made a very loud bang and another pony, standing only metres away, took fright and reared suddenly. The rider was taken completely by surprise and he fell

from the saddle as the pony panicked and bolted.

Without a rider in the saddle to stop him, the pony dashed across the arena, scattering everyone in its path. Several screams rang out as the runaway pony circled the arena looking for a way out.

'Now look what you've done!' scowled Emma.

Most of the audience quickly jumped to its feet as the frightened creature headed towards a gap in the roped off enclosure near Emma and Sheltie. Emma could see that if the pony made it to the exit, it would be right on top of the crowds. It had to be stopped.

Emma urged Sheltie forward. They blocked the exit and faced the oncoming pony. The pony looked scared and wild. But Sheltie wasn't frightened. The little Shetland stood his ground as the charging pony galloped towards them.

Emma felt really nervous. She could see the fear in the pony's eyes and didn't know what she was going to do next.

Luckily, Sheltie knew exactly what to do. Just as the pony was almost upon them, Sheltie raised his head and gave a shrill whinny. Suddenly the runaway stopped in his tracks.

The pony now stood before them as quiet as a lamb, looking around for its owner.

Emma slipped gently from the saddle and caught hold of the pony's loose rein. The poor thing was trembling with fright.

'Thanks,' said the boy as he calmed down his pony and stroked its neck. 'It was a good job you were there. That little pony of yours must have nerves of steel!'

Once all the excitement was over and the pony had been led away, Mrs Brandon appeared and began organizing everyone into their groups.

Both players and audience were waiting for the Bicklington Battlers.

The scene was set. The incident with the runaway pony was soon forgotten and the battle was about to begin.

Chapter Nine

Prince John and his knights won their battle against the enemy. The crowds yelled and cheered as the soldiers fought, jabbing at shields with axes and spears.

Swords clashed and actors fell to the ground, one by one, pretending to be dead. Prince John raised his banner in victory.

The jousting display which followed

was spectacular. Knights in shining armour rode against each other with long lances. The horses thundered along as the riders tried to knock each other off.

'Isn't it fantastic!' said Emma. She hugged Sheltie in excitement as the display came to an end. Flags waved and the cast and actors marched past to collect their applause.

Mrs Brandon suddenly became busy sorting out the procession line for the grand parade, which was coming next.

Everyone wearing costumes took up their places and positions. The band was already playing softly.

Sally was right up at the front with Prince John and Melody. But Melody seemed to be having trouble with Sapphire.

Although Emma and Sheltie were right at the very back of the line, by leaning out, Emma could see all the way up to the front. And she could see Sapphire hopping about and skipping sideways out of line.

'That's odd, Sheltie,' said Emma. 'Melody's such a good rider. It's not like *her* to let Sapphire play up like that.'

Sheltie looked too, and watched with Emma as Sapphire danced and sidestepped in a wild, skittish manner. Sapphire just didn't seem to want to stand still. Even when Melody gathered him in on a tight rein, the pony was restless and bursting to get going.

The grand parade was about to start. Mrs Brandon was hurrying along the line, checking everyone's positions.

As she reached the head of the procession, she gave the signal for the parade to begin. The band began to play more loudly and the procession moved forward, slowly, in step to the marching music. Everyone seemed perfect, except for Melody and Sapphire. The pony had become really nervous of the drumbeats and was trying to surge ahead of the parade, away from the band.

Then two cymbals crashed together and it proved too much for Sapphire. Melody couldn't hold the pony any longer. She barely managed to stay in the saddle as Sapphire shot forward and streaked off across the meadow.

Sally gasped as pony and rider left the head of the parade and galloped away into the distance.

Emma and Sheltie watched too from the back of the line. They couldn't believe it either. Then suddenly Mrs

Brandon was flapping her arms and waving to Emma, yelling, 'Quickly, Emma! Bring Sheltie up to the front!'

Emma didn't have to be asked twice. She squeezed with her legs and Sheltie trotted right up to the front of the line.

'Right,' said Mrs Brandon. She sounded as if she was used to emergencies. 'A slight change of plan. Sally, you ride first escort in front of Prince John and Casper. Emma, you ride Sheltie just ahead and lead the parade.'

Emma couldn't believe her ears. 'Lead the parade!' she gasped.

'Yes,' smiled Mrs Brandon. 'After seeing Sheltie stand his ground in the path of that runaway pony, I think he will be up to it, don't you?'

'I *know* he will be,' beamed Emma. 'Come on, Sheltie!'

The parade continued, with Emma and Sheltie right up at the very front, heading the procession. Emma glanced back at Sally, who was grinning from ear to ear.

Emma felt so proud, leading the

grand parade across the field and
down into the village.

Everyone cheered and waved as
they passed.

The band played loudly and the
cymbals crashed, but Sheltie didn't
flinch once. The little Shetland pony

marched forward, lifting his hoofs high and tossing his head in time to the music.

Sheltie's feather danced and bobbed as he marched through the village.

Even when some of the crowd blew whistles, Sheltie didn't mind. He was enjoying leading the parade as much as Emma was.

They led the procession all round the village, up and down the high street, then back to the meadow.

Dad was there the whole time with his video camera. And so was the local television station. They were filming the parade for the evening news.

When it was all over, and Emma was back at home watching it again on TV with Mum, Dad and Joshua, she felt just as excited.

Suddenly the whole television screen was filled with an image of Sheltie in his costume, complete with dancing feather bobbing in time to the music.

'Wheee!' squealed Joshua as he pointed at the television. 'Sheltie, Sheltie, Sheltie.' He wriggled so much that he almost bounced off Mum's lap.

Emma laughed with glee and hugged her knees. She hoped Sally was watching at home.

'I wonder what happened to Melody,' said Dad.

'She's probably reached Summerland Bay by now,' joked Mum. 'I've never seen a pony rush off at such a gallop.'

'Well, I hope she managed to stop before she hit the sea,' grinned Emma.

Just at that moment, the television camera passed across the watching crowds. And there, standing on the sidelines was a very bedraggled Melody. She was covered from head to foot in sticky mud and looking very sorry for herself as Sheltie pranced by.

'Look!' yelled Emma, pointing at the screen. 'It's Melody.'

'Now you know what happened to her,' joked Mum. 'She rushed off to have a mud bath!'

Mum didn't mean to be unkind, but it did sound funny. And everyone laughed so loudly that even Sheltie could hear them outside in his paddock. The little Shetland pony threw up his head and blew the biggest raspberry that Little Applewood had ever heard.